Welcome!

Dear Reader,

Welcome to a world of imagination!

My First Story was designed for 5-7 year-olds as an introduction to creative writing and to promote an enjoyment of reading and writing from an early age.

The simple, fun storyboards give even the youngest and most reluctant writers the chance to become interested in literacy by giving them a framework within which to shape their ideas. Pupils could also choose to write without the storyboards, allowing older children to let their creativity flow as much as possible, encouraging the use of imagination and descriptive language.

We believe that seeing their work in print will inspire a love of reading and writing and give these young writers the confidence to develop their skills in the future.

There is nothing like the imagination of children, and this is reflected in the creativity and individuality of the stories in this anthology. I hope you'll enjoy reading their first stories as much as we have.

Jenni Bannister

Editorial Manager

Ima ine. .

Each child was given the beginning of a story and
then chose one of five storyboards, using the pictures
and their imagination to complete the tale. You can
view the storyboards at the end of this book.

The Beginning...

One night Ellie was woken by a tapping at her window.

It was Spencer the elf! 'Would you like to go on an adventure?' he asked.

They flew above the rooftops. Soon they had arrived...

Adventures From The South West

Contents

Emelia Wagstaff (6) 62

Charlestown Primary School, St. Austell

Teigan Spry (6) 63
Layla Dotty Walby (5) 64
Khloe Chapman (5) 65
Dougie Wallace (6) 66
Kieran James (6) 67
Luca Dominic Vercoe (5) 68
Nicholas Ling (5) 69
Naomi Squire (6) 70
Oliver Ferguson (6) 71
Millie Dailey (5) 72
Lucas Woodcock (6) 73
Dylan Rundle (5) 74
Calum Matthew Knowles (6) 75
Bella Ayling (6) 76
Milly Frances Sanders-Hulme (6) 77
Lola Mae Butters (6) 78
Sophie Leigh Stoddern (6) 79
Isabelle Martin (6) 80

King's Park Academy, Bournemouth

Amina Marie Moore Webb (7) 81
Keytlin Zapata (7) 82
Lincoln Jack Eldergill (7) 84
Maja Grzelczak (7) 86
Summer Marie Casserly (7) 88
Mia Williams (7) 90
Jacob mpho Orson (7) 92
Naomi Rachel Badger (7) 94
Grace Anthony-Ince (7) 95
Musa Balajo (7) 96
Lily Tebboth (7) 97
Alicja Lewandowska (7) 98
Zalaa Shinwari (7) 99
Caleb Morrison (7) 100
Jessica Pardy (7) 101
Rihanna Jordan Banes (7) 102
Olivia Aitken (6) 103
Liam Clark (6) 104

Callum Jones (7) 105
Vanessa Kate Muzanenhamo (7) 106
Shahid Mahmoodi (7) 108
Maud Lowe (6) 109
Greta (7) 110
Maison Walkinshaw (7) 111
Rubie Barnes (7) 112
Leyla Tuanna Kilic (6) 113
Nasrine Tir (7) 114
Ugnius Stankus (7) 115
Valentina Vallejos (7) 116
Meyra Guler Acik (7) 117
Lucy Downton (7) 118
Leo George Bekir (7) 119
Antonia Elcock (7) 120
Jana Anna Zirne (7) 121
Millie Taylor (7) 122
Joanna Maru (7) 123
Amber Moors (7) 124
Patryk Wieczorek (6) 125
Roxy Hardman (7) 126
Alfie Jhon Maunder (7) 127
Chloe Forbes (7) 128
Grace Wigmore (7) 129
Nataliya Marguerite Le Notre (7) 130

Priestley Primary School, Calne

Heidi Ainge (6) 131
Riley Ewart George Green (7) 132
Elliott Mouillé (6) 133
Ffion Simpkins (6) 134
Abigail Wright (6) 135

The Stories

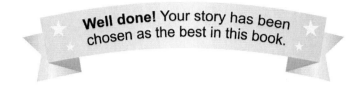

Well done! Your story has been chosen as the best in this book.

Harry's Jungle Story

Suddenly, Ellie was swinging on thorny vines. She landed on the ground and walked through green and brown leaves.

Then she met a vicious snake. She felt nervous, she thought she should run away but she was too scared to move.The snake hissed. She ran away and hid in a green bush. Soon the snake passed and she was safe.

But a lion found her! She had never seen a lion before. She thought the lion would be scary but he wasn't. The lion offered her a ride on his back. It was exciting and fun.

Soon it was time to go home. She swung on thorny vines all the way home.

Harry Blundell (6)

Bristol Grammar Lower School, Bristol

Kitty's Zoo Story

They arrived at Pixie's Zoo. 'Spencer, how did you know I loved the zoo?' said Ellie.

'It's not just any zoo,' said Spencer.

At that moment, 'Hello Spencer!' said the humongous grey elephant. 'Would you like me to show you around?'

'Yes please!' said Ellie, looking rather puzzled. 'Spencer, it can talk!'

'Hop on,' said the Henry the elephant. They strolled through the zoo, smiling as they went.

'It's a very nice view up here,' said Ellie, 'but I can't quite see over the bamboo.'

'Pandas!' squealed Beth, Ellie's bear.

'Aah!' gasped Ellie. 'Beth is talking.'

Beth jumped off Henry's trunk and disappeared. 'Follow her,' said Ellie.

On the other side of the bamboo they found a large black and white panda called Po. She had Beth in her arms. Ellie wondered if Po knew it was Beth and not Stephanie, her cub. At that moment Spencer arrived cuddling sweet, adorable Stephanie.

'I think this belongs to you,' said Spencer.

'Then who's this?' said Po.

'It's my teddy,' said Ellie. 'Please could I have it back?' asked Ellie.

'Yes you may,' said Po.

At that moment there was the sound of bamboo rustling. It was Henry.

'It's time to go,' he said. Off they went, marching through the zoo. Spencer pointed out all of the amazing animals as they passed. Henry made sure he held on tight to Beth so she wouldn't escape again. Ellie's tummy started to rumble.

'I'm so hungry!' said Ellie.

'I know someone who might be able to help you,' said Henry. Henry took them to see Miles the monkey.

Miles was a big, cheeky monkey. He really loved bananas. 'Do you want one?' asked Miles, 'I've got a secret stash.'

'Yes please. I'm starving!' said Ellie, 'these bananas are so delicious!' Meanwhile Beth was having plenty of fun, playing on the vines.

'Your banana is much bigger than mine,' said Ellie.

'I know, that's because I'm much bigger than you,' said Miles with a smile.

'It's time to go now,' said Henry.

'Bye Miles, thank you for the banana,' said Ellie.
Henry took Ellie back home.
'Thank you for a wonderful night,' said Ellie. 'I've
had a fantastic time.' Ellie waved goodbye when
Henry strolled away carrying Spencer on his back.

Kitty Newman (7)
Antony CE Primary School, Torpoint

Keira's Jungle Story

They arrived in a mystery land that they thought was a jungle. They hung on vines.

When they reached for the next vine it was a snake! The snake had his name spelt down his neck. It was Agro Dan! He was angry!

He started chasing them. They ran really fast. Spencer said, 'Run fast, run faster Ellie!'

Then they bumped into a lion. Luckily it was a friendly lion that asked them, 'Do you want a tour?'

'Yes please!' they said.

'Jump on then, here is the monkey.'

The monkey was swinging in the trees. Then he did a silly dance. He threw two bananas down, one for Ellie and the other for Spencer.

Then they jumped onto a vine and swung like the monkey. Where did they swing next? Who knows?

Keira Brown (7)
Antony CE Primary School, Torpoint

Saskia's Zoo Story

They arrived at the zoo. Spencer said, 'Come on, let's explore.'

'Yay,' said Ellie.

'Come on then!' said Spencer.

First they saw an elephant that said, 'Do you want me to take you round the whole zoo?'

'Yes please!' said Spencer and Ellie.

'First I will take you to Izzy the panda,' said the elephant.

As they walked they saw a bamboo forest and that was when they met Izzy the panda; he was scoffing down some bamboo.

'Hi Izzy,' said Ellie, 'do you want to hold my teddy?'

'Yes please,' said Izzy.

'Your baby is really cute,' said Spencer.

'Thanks,' said Izzy.

'We have to go now, bye!' said Ellie.

'Next I will take you to Max the monkey,' said the elephant.

'I love monkeys!' said Ellie. As they walked they went through a jungle. Then they saw Max!

'Hi Max!' said Ellie. 'Why are you eating a banana?' asked Ellie.

'Because they are my favourite food,' said Max, 'do you want one?'

'Yes please!' said Ellie.

'Time to go,' said Spencer.

'OK,' said Ellie.

Once they got home Ellie said goodbye and waved. Ellie walked into her house, she went upstairs and got back into bed.

Saskia Brisley (7)

Antony CE Primary School, Torpoint

Frankie's Magical Story

They met a beautiful unicorn called Rainbow, her fur was as white as snow and her horn was all the colours of the rainbow. They hopped onto her back to go on their adventure.

Along the way they came across Dragon Valley. The landscape was dark and scary and had a volcano erupting hot lava!

Then they came across a dragon who was enormous and purple with long, sharp teeth. He blew fire at them.

They ran away from the dragon but it chased after them. Rainbow swooped down to get them and they climbed onto her back. They were shaking with fear, but Ellie had her teddy called Softy, with her.

They were travelling for a while in the sky. It was pink and the clouds were fluffy like marshmallows: wait, they were marshmallows! Where was Rainbow taking them?

Rainbow swiftly landed. 'Welcome to Candy Island.' They loved exploring it, there were lollipop trees, lemonade lakes and gingerbread houses. All of a sudden there was a witch named Esmerelda. 'Eat as much as you like!' she said.

After all the candy and lemonade, Ellie's tummy was full. 'It is time to go to bed,' said Spencer.

Frankie Mae Fryer (6)
Antony CE Primary School, Torpoint

Grace's Pirate Story

They arrived in a boat. The sea was sparkling bright blue and the sun was shining. They were close to an island with palm trees and coconuts. They thought they should land there as the clouds were gathering.

They found a treasure chest. Ellie stood on it and her bear put on a crown she'd found by the chest. Ellie was happy but Spencer was not. He could see a ship in the distance!

A grumpy old pirate with a big black beard, a parrot, a pegleg, a cutlass and a hook kidnapped them. He said, 'If you don't do what I say I'll make you walk the plank! Argh!'

Spencer shouted as he walked the plank, 'Ellie! Don't let him make you walk the plank! I don't think anything will save us. Aaaah!' But there was a dolphin playing around the ship.

Spencer was wrong. The dolphins saved them! They had a wild ride back to the island.

They rowed back to the path. It was almost time for tea.

'I hope you had a lovely time. I wonder what adventure we will have next time. Bye Ellie!'

Grace Rose Lentell (6)
Antony CE Primary School, Torpoint

Chloe's Magical Story

They flew through the cloud garden on Violet, the magical pony. Ellie, Spencer and Violet landed in Rainbow Land. Rainbow Land was full of beautiful colours and sweet smelling flowers.

It was very peaceful and quiet until a fire-breathing dragon appeared. Smoky the dragon was very cross and he chased the children.

Smoky scared the children, they ran as fast as they could to escape. The children found Violet eating nearby and jumped on her back. Violet flew them all to safety.

'Luckily Violet was there to save us,' said Ellie.

'Yes,' said Spencer, 'she flies very fast.' The children slid down Violet's back to give her a rest.

As Violet went to drink from Rainbow River, the children met a kind lady called Chloe. Chloe had lots of yummy treats and lollipops that she shared with everyone.

The children told Chloe about scary old Smoky and how he chased them. Chloe wanted to cheer the children up so she let them ride her broomstick all the way home.

Chloe Matthews (7)

Antony CE Primary School, Torpoint

Aaron's Magical Story

They arrived at Unicorn Land where magical things happen. Everything was so colourful and shiny! Even the unicorns were nice. Spencer shouted, 'Hop on, we can have a ride!' to Ellie.

Ellie and Spencer landed in a place where dragons are not so friendly. He looked angry. They shouted, 'Run before he gets us!'

Both of them turned around and ran for their lives. 'Run as fast as you can!' shouted Spencer.

Suddenly the unicorn appeared and whizzed them off to Lollipop Land. Everything there was made from lollipops. Everything was made of sweets, even the grass!

All of a sudden a witch appeared, she told them to go to her house.

Spencer the elf's broomstick heard what had happened. It saved them. They both jumped on and went back to Ellie's house.

Aaron Wills (7)

Antony CE Primary School, Torpoint

Bella's Magical Story

They arrived in the magical world that was called Fairytale Land. There were unicorns and magical people.

Then a fierce dragon appeared. Ellie was really scared. 'Keep away from my nest!' shouted the dragon.

They ran and ran until they couldn't run any further and then the dragon made a loud *roar!*

'Oh no, what are we going to do?' cried Ellie.

Suddenly, out of the clouds came a unicorn. They quickly climbed on her back and rode off.

Later the unicorn turned into a bad witch because she had tricked them. 'You must stay here forever!' said the witch.

When the witch wasn't looking they grabbed her broomstick and escaped back home.

Bella Gray (6)
Antony CE Primary School, Torpoint

Esmé's Magical Story

They arrived in the Land of Dragons and Unicorns. Ellie said, 'Look! I see a red and white unicorn. Let's go and see it.' Spencer and Ellie rode the unicorn for a while.

Suddenly they saw a big dragon and it was very scary! It had red, orange and yellow flames coming from its mouth.

It started to chase them and the little bear was getting tired. Ellie had to pick her up. After that they sat under a big tree and started to climb it.

Just then the unicorn appeared again. She invited Spencer and Ellie to the Land of Sweets and Good Witches.

They met a witch who seemed quite scary to them but she was nice. She gave them some sweeties and they were yummy.

At the end the witch let them have a go on her broomstick to fly home.

Esmé Rundle (7)
Antony CE Primary School, Torpoint

Ava's Magical Story

They arrived in a magical forest. They met a princess unicorn called Glamour. They went for a ride on Princess Glamour through the magical forest.

Ellie and Spencer got off Princess Glamour and saw a huge fire-breathing dragon. They were so scared that they screamed!

They got so scared, Ellie and Spencer ran away because the fire-breathing dragon blew so hard and lots of fire came out.

They got back on Princess Glamour and went to a house made out of candy. It belonged to a witch. The witch came out of the house made of candy and was really friendly. The witch gave them lots and lots of candy.

The witch lent Ellie and Spencer her broomstick. They flew home and Glamour followed them.

Ava Richards (7)
Antony CE Primary School, Torpoint

Michael's Magical Story

They landed on a magical land. 'Wow! It's a unicorn! Let's ride it. We're in the air! There's a rainbow behind the unicorn,' said Ellie.

The unicorn led them to a dragon, it was trying to hurt them. It could breathe fire.

'Let's run!' said Spencer. 'Argh! Run! Quick! He's behind us!'

They were back with the unicorn. Then they were in the air again. There was a rainbow behind the unicorn.

The unicorn left them with a witch. 'Let's run with her broom!' said Ellie.

They were in the air on a broom. 'Thank you for the adventure!' said Ellie.

Michael Philip Stevens (7)
Antony CE Primary School, Torpoint

Amber's Magical Story

They arrived in a magical land called Unicornia. Ellie and Spencer discovered a pretty, magic unicorn.

Once they had finished their magical ride they saw a fire-breathing dragon.

Spencer tried to use his magic on the dragon but it made the dragon very angry.

Spencer and Ellie's unicorn friend picked them up, rescuing them from the evil dragon.

Then their dragon friend mysteriously vanished.

The witch looked bad, she was actually Ellie's mummy in disguise!

The witch was very kind, she lent them her broomstick to fly home.

Amber Smith (6)
Antony CE Primary School, Torpoint

Erin's Magical Story

They arrived in a magical land where there were unicorns.

They saw a magical dragon. They were frightened of dragons. It was a very fierce dragon with fire coming out of its mouth.

They ran away screaming because the dragon was chasing them.

They ran into a magical unicorn. She had a magical unicorn horn and she was all pink.

They also saw a scary witch wearing a purple cape. They thought that she was a nasty witch but she wasn't.

The kind witch gave them her flying broomstick. They flew away home.

Erin Cameron Davies (6)

Antony CE Primary School, Torpoint

Darcie Drew's Magical Story

They arrived at a magical land. They found a unicorn and decided that they would ride it.

Then there came a dragon. The dragon saw them and got angry. They ran away and escaped.

As they were running Teddy fell over. They had to quickly pick him up.

The unicorn grabbed them and ran really quickly.

Then they met a nice witch, her name was Winnie the Witch.

Winnie the Witch let them ride her broomstick home.

Darcie Drew Harris (7)

Antony CE Primary School, Torpoint

Chloe's Jungle Story

They swung through on the trees. They swung through mountains, seas and soon they arrived at the jungle.

When they arrived a snake came along and said, 'I am going to eat you!' in a slithery voice.

The snake tried to follow them but they were too fast.

Finally they were saved by a lion. The snake still followed so they tried to hide.

The lion let them ride on his back and they were saved. They swung back home.

Chloe Marie Brannan (6)

Antony CE Primary School, Torpoint

Untitled

They arrived in a forest, there were thousands of trees. There were lots of leaves and lots of scary sounds.

It was very wet in the rainforest.

Then it was very sunny in the rainforest so they could walk in the rainforest.

It was a nice windy day to play with kites.

It was a sunny day, they ran round in the beautiful rainforest.

Then it was rainy.

Nathan Roberts (7)

Boskenwyn School, Helston

Jessica's Space Story

'Wow!' said Ellie, 'this is amazing fun!' She could not believe her sparkling eyes. She couldn't believe what she saw ahead of her. A beautiful white moon!

They saw an alien behind them. 'Wow! What is that?' said Ellie.

'I don't know,' said Spencer.

An alien looked at a button in his spaceship. He pressed it. They got sucked up like a hoover.

They took off and set off for home. Ellie smiled and looked down...

A tongue touched the bottom of the ship. 'Quick!' They managed to get away quickly.

Unfortunately, they had to say goodbye. 'Bye,' said Spencer. Ellie went home and went to bed.

Jessica Moore (6)

Brighstone CE Aided Primary School, Newport

Matilda's Space Story

They flew off into the starry sky. Ellie clutched
Spencer's hand. Ellie was excited.

They landed with a *crash, bang, boom*. 'Quick!' said
Ellie. They gazed at the shimmering stars.

An alien called Green followed them. He sent down
a beam of light. Ellie zoomed into the spaceship.
She waved and cheered to the other aliens. She
was kind to the alien who wanted to be friends
with her.

Suddenly a tongue shot out from a monster's
mouth.

'Yuck!' said Ellie, 'what's there?'

They zoomed off into the dark sky. They flew off to
Ellie's home. She waved goodbye.

Matilda Green (6)
Brighstone CE Aided Primary School, Newport

Lily's Space Story

Ellie was squeezing the elf's hand. As quick as a
flash they flew away.
Ellie was happy. Suddenly, Ellie saw a pink alien
and the alien said, 'Hi.'
Soon Ellie and her teddy got sucked up. Ellie felt
upset because she was by herself.
Suddenly, Ellie zoomed away. She felt happy.
Suddenly, a wet tongue appeared. It was an alien's
tongue.
'I can see the alien!' said the elf. 'Bye!' said the elf.
Ellie went home.

Lily Rogers (6)
Brighstone CE Aided Primary School, Newport

Arianwen's Space Story

Ellie clutched her teddy tightly because she was a little bit scared. 'Are we nearly there?' asked Ellie but Spencer didn't answer.

All of a sudden Ellie heard a giggle. She turned around. Just then Spencer saw an alien. 'Hee, hee!' gurgled the alien.

Just then Ellie heard a noise. Ellie looked up. The light shone right through Ellie's eyes. Just when Ellie was about to run away she flew up to a spaceship.

Ellie flew all around the world in the alien's spaceship. 'Best day ever!' shouted Ellie.

All of a sudden something hit the spaceship. 'What's that?' asked Ellie. It was a monster's tongue.

Ellie hopped out of the spaceship. 'Goodbye alien!' Ellie had a really fun day!

Arianwen Craig (6)
Brighstone CE Aided Primary School, Newport

Tilly's Space Story

Ellie was awoken by a noise. She flew out of the window and they flew to the moon.

Ellie was excited. In the corner of Ellie's eye Ellie saw an alien. Ellie was shocked.

Ellie looked up and Ellie's teddy did as well. Ellie called, 'Goodbye!' to the elf.

Ellie and the alien zoomed through space. Ellie saw shining stars.

Suddenly, a huge monster bumped into the spaceship. Ellie was scared.

Ellie was home at last. 'Goodbye,' said Ellie. Ellie was happy at last. How did Ellie breathe in space?

Tilly Margaret Brodie (6)

Brighstone CE Aided Primary School, Newport

Gemma's Space Story

Ellie squeezed out of the window and flew out into space.

They softly landed on the smooth moon and out of the corner of Ellie's eye she saw an alien. She was frightened. She didn't know what to do.

Ellie saw a speck of light in the corner of her eye. It was sucking up Ellie. It was an alien.

They zoomed and zoomed until they stopped. 'That was an adventure!' said Ellie.

On the side of the spaceship was an alien licking it.

They stopped by Ellie's house and she hopped out quietly.

Gemma Louise Davis (6)
Brighstone CE Aided Primary School, Newport

Ava's Space Story

One night Ellie heard a tapping. The little girl saw an elf. He clutched her hand.
The elf took her up to the moon. She saw the stars shining at her.
When Ellie saw a light on top of her she got sucked up.
After that the alien took off to the stars.
Then a huge alien tried to eat the ship but it didn't get eaten by it.
After that the alien took Ellie back to her house.

Ava Marie Downer (5)
Brighstone CE Aided Primary School, Newport

Jack's Space Story

Ellie and Spencer saw stars. Ellie found a moon with an alien on it.

Ellie picked stars. They saw an alien look up to the sky at a big spaceship. Ellie went into the big ship. She floated up to the spaceship.

Then she floated back home.

There was an enormous big monster who almost ate the ship.

After they had got back home Ellie played with the stars.

Jack Fisher (5)

Brighstone CE Aided Primary School, Newport

Tobin's Space Story

The elf held the little girl's hand. She didn't like it.
Suddenly the little girl saw an alien.
The little girl got sucked up. The little girl was frightened.
The little girl got into the spaceship.
She saw a monster. The monster almost ate the ship.
The spaceship dropped the girl off and she waved goodbye.

Tobin Howard (6)

Brighstone CE Aided Primary School, Newport

Soul's Space Story

Ellie was flying with the boy. Ellie saw she was flying.

Then Ellie saw an alien, it was on the moon.

Ellie saw that the flashing alien had a spaceship.

Then Ellie was about to go home, she went to Earth.

Ellie then saw a big monster. He had a big tongue.

Ellie finally got home.

Soul Taylor (6)

Brighstone CE Aided Primary School, Newport

Izzy's Space Story

Ellie looked up to the stars above. She heard a beeping sound coming from the sky above.
They said goodbye.
The alien said, 'Up you go!'
Ellie said, 'I love you to the moon and back.'
There was a big monster. Up, up it went.
They said, 'I love you.'

Izzy Rogers (6)

Brighstone CE Aided Primary School, Newport

Ettienne's Space Story

Ellie and Spencer flew to the moon.
Ellie saw the alien out of the corner of her eye.
Ellie got sucked up by the alien.
'Thank you Alien!' said Ellie.
The alien pressed a button.
'Goodbye!' said Ellie.

Ettienne McKay (6)
Brighstone CE Aided Primary School, Newport

Sienna's Space Story

Spencer clutched Ellie's hand tightly. Both of them had crashed. 'Ellie, have you landed OK? Let's take some stars home. I will put them in my pocket,' said Spencer.

Out of the corner of Ellie's eye was an alien.

The alien pressed a sparkly button. Ellie went up in the spaceship.

'Why is there another spaceship following us?' she asked. 'Argh a monster! That was close,' said Ellie. Ellie waved goodbye.

Sienna Attrill (6)

Brighstone CE Aided Primary School, Newport

Jack's Jungle Story

Suddenly, the next thing Ellie knew, she was swinging on vines. Then she saw that her teddy was alive.

Then they met a vicious and scary snake. Just then the snake tried to eat them.

They ran away. They ran as fast as they could, deeper into the jungle.

Then they stumbled into a friendly lion. The lion said to them, 'Would you like to ride on my back?'

'Yes,' they said.

'Hop on then!' he said.

'Thank you for letting us ride on your back to some vines. We can swing to get home.'

When they got home, Ellie told her mum and dad about her adventure.

Jack Bradley (6)
Bristol Grammar Lower School, Bristol

Bea's Jungle Story

Suddenly Ellie was swinging across fresh green vines. Teddy swung across the vines as well.
Oh no! Suddenly a ginormous snake slithered out of a bush.
'Oh no, I'm frightened!' said Ellie.
They ran as fast as they could. Finally they were okay! Teddy ran too.
Suddenly a lion pounced out of a bush! The lion asked if they wanted to have a ride.
The lion ran very fast and soon they saw the end of the forest.
Soon they were back on the vines and they swung back home.

Bea Hogg (6)
Bristol Grammar Lower School, Bristol

Noah's Jungle Story

The first thing they saw was their hands on the vines. Then they started to swing on it.

They were shocked to meet a huge, ferocious rattlesnake. Just then the rattlesnake tried to eat them.

After that the rattlesnake tried to hypnotise them, but they got away, just in the nick of time!

As they got deeper into the forest they met a really kind lion hiding in the leaves.

They both wanted to know how fast the lion was so they both asked if they could ride on his back.

After the ride had finished they swung on some vines, all the way back home.

Noah Wragg (6)

Bristol Grammar Lower School, Bristol

Coco's Jungle Story

Suddenly Ellie was swinging on the amazing vines with her best friend ever.

Just then they met a vicious snake and they were frightened by the fierce snake.

Then they ran as fast as they could before the fierce snake was about to eat them whole.

Luckily they met the king lion. They were scared at first but then they got along.

Then the lion took them home. Ellie and Spencer had never been on a lion's back before.

Finally they swung back on the vines. They told their mum and dad all about their adventure.

Coco Beavis (6)

Bristol Grammar Lower School, Bristol

Oliver's Jungle Story

The next thing Ellie knew, she was hanging from a vine with her teddy.

Just then they met a slimy snake and he coiled himself around a branch.

Suddenly they turned and ran away from the snake and Ellie's teddy ran behind them.

Then they met a friendly lion with very, very, very big, dirty fangs.

They had a ride on the lion's back. They wanted to see how fast the lion was.

Then they swung back home. Ellie told her mum and dad about it all.

Oliver James Burchell (6)

Bristol Grammar Lower School, Bristol

Olly's Jungle Story

Suddenly Ellie found herself swinging on a vine with Spencer and her teddy.

Then they met a slimy snake and he curled around a branch.

Suddenly the snake chased them and they all ran away.

Then they met a friendly lion with big, sharp claws.

He kindly let them ride on his back in the spiky, prickly bushes and tall, long grass.

At last it was getting dark and they were getting tired. Finally they said goodbye to the lion and they swung back home.

Olly Woolford (6)

Bristol Grammar Lower School, Bristol

Yousef's Jungle Story

They arrived in the jungle. Lots of creatures surrounded them. The gorillas taught Ellie to swing on vines. She was having lots of fun.
Then they met a snake.
The snake chased them until they tripped. *Cling! Bang! Boom!* They fell into a bush. The snake couldn't see them. Thankfully the snake went the wrong way.
Then they met a lion.
The lion carried them back home.
Once again they swung on vines.

Yousef Naaisa (6)
Bristol Grammar Lower School, Bristol

Eva's Jungle Story

Suddenly Ellie found herself swinging on long green vines.

But then Ellie found a long, green, vicious boa constrictor!

The snake rose up and opened his mouth, as if to eat them.

But then they met a big, friendly lion.

Suddenly they jumped onto the lion's back and set off.

Finally they returned back home.

Eva Wragg (6)

Bristol Grammar Lower School, Bristol

Anais' Jungle Story

Suddenly Ellie was on a vine, swinging across the river.
Then they met a nasty snake and he rose up, about to eat them. Then the snake chased them.
Suddenly, they met a tiger.
He said 'Do you want a ride?'
Next they jumped on his back. It was fun.
Finally they went swinging home.

Anais Lucia Gillings (6)
Bristol Grammar Lower School, Bristol

Rufus' Jungle Story

Suddenly Ellie was swinging on long vines. It was fun.

The snake was very scary. They had no idea what to do. They ran away from the snake. He tried to get them but he couldn't.

Then they found a lovely lion. He was hiding in a bush. They rode the lion. It was very fun. They had never been on a lion's back through the jungle.

Finally, Ellie got back home. She told her dad and her mum about her adventure.

Rufus Hull (6)

Bristol Grammar Lower School, Bristol

Harriet's Zoo Story

They arrived at an amazing zoo! Spencer held
Ellie's hand and walked with her through the gate.
'I'm quite nervous, what if I fall off an animal?'
shouted Ellie.

'You will be fine,' said Spencer.

Spencer took Ellie on an elephant ride. Ellie closed
her eyes. 'You can open up your eyes now,'
whispered Spencer.

'Wow, this is quite fun!' Ellie said.

'I told you!' shouted Spencer. 'This is Spotty,' said
Spencer, 'he loves everyone.'

'Ha, ha, ha, he's so fluffy!' shouted Ellie, 'I love him
so much!'

'I do too,' whispered Spencer.

Then they went back on the elephant. They passed
lions, tigers, bears, polar bears, grizzly bears and
all sorts of animals in the animal jungle.

Then they saw a monkey. They ate bananas and
had a hug. Then they went back on the elephant.
'It's time to go home,' said Spencer.

'OK,' said Ellie.

Harriet Hodgson (6)
Buckholme Towers School, Poole

Ben's Pirate Story

They were at the beach. 'I want to find some gold,' Ellie said.

'Yes we will,' said Spencer. Soon they arrived at the island. They wanted to explore the island and Ellie started to dig.

'I wonder...' said Spencer.

'I'm scared,' said Ellie.

A large boat came sailing in. 'What's that?' yelled Spencer. It was a pirate ship. Ellie was standing on the treasure chest.

'Who's that stealing my treasure?' asked a pirate.

'It's only me and him,' said Ellie.

'You are arrested for stealing my treasure,' said the pirate. 'Arrrggh!' said the pirate. 'You can have three coins each and you my girl can have a necklace. You can both go on my ship. Do you want to have some rum?'

'No thank you,' said Spencer. 'I am not really a pirate.'

'You have to walk the plank!' said the pirate.

'I hate walking planks!' said Spencer.

'But you have to because you took my treasure!' said the pirate.

Soon there were two dolphins. Ellie and Spencer got a dolphin each. The dolphins whistled and the air was fresh. The sea was clear.

They went home and Ellie went to bed. She had a dream about pirates.

Benjamin Babb (6)

Buckholme Towers School, Poole

Esme's Zoo Story

They arrived at the wild zoo. Spencer the elf grabbed Ellie's hand. 'I love zoos!' shouted Ellie. Nearly, everyone heard Ellie shout. 'I hope we see pandas,' said Ellie.

Then Spencer the elf carried Ellie and put her on the elephant. Spencer rode the elephant to the panda.

The panda's name was Sophie. She had babies. Spencer held one and Ellie wanted to hold one of the pandas. Then she saw the hungry crocodiles. The soft cats were in a cage.

Then she saw a snake. Then the animals stopped, there were no more. 'Shall we go and find some more animals!' asked Spencer.

'Yes!' said Ellie.

'There are the monkeys, I want to stay here all night,' said Ellie.

'But where are you going to sleep?' asked Spencer.

'Oh yes, I do not know,' she said.

'It's hometime now,' said Spencer.

All night Ellie dreamed about what adventure she was going to have.

Esme Johnson (6)
Buckholme Towers School, Poole

Grace's Adventure Story

Soon they had arrived at Cloud Land!

'Look, there's Cloud Horse! Hop on!' said Spencer. Cloud Land was a wonderful place. Everything was made out of clouds! Ellie hopped onto a bouncing cloud. Spencer didn't, he was afraid of heights and bouncy clouds. They made people who bounced on them go really high. Then they heard a noise.

'What's that noise?' asked Ellie. Spencer shivered.

'It's a cloud dragon,' said Spencer. Ellie's eye caught something.

'What's that?' asked Ellie.

'A cloud ball!' shouted Spencer. 'Cloud dragons are scared of cloud balls.' They threw lots of cloud balls at the cloud dragon but nothing happened. Then Spencer saw two cloud swords. He handed one to Ellie. They managed to kill the dragon. Then, the cloud queen appeared, 'You two have been very brave,' she said, 'but I think it's time Ellie goes now.' Spencer took her home.

'You'll come again won't you?' asked Ellie.

'Of course,' said Spencer, 'goodnight.'

Grace Elizabeth Rae Upshall (7)

Buckholme Towers School, Poole

Harley's Pirate Story

They arrived at Treasure Island. There were pirates around. 'Let's get out of here!' shouted Spencer. They ran away!

'Let's get digging!' shouted Ellie.

'No!' said Spencer, 'the captain is all around!'

'See!' said Ellie, 'he is here!'

'No he isn't,' said Spencer.

'Yes he is,' said Ellie.

'Arr me hearties, give me back my treasure or else I will cut your heads off!' said the pirate. 'I'm going to make you walk the plank now you scallywags.' One by one they fell off.

Two dolphins popped up and they saved their lives. Spencer and Ellie arrived back home and Spencer dreamed of his lovely day.

Harley Gill (6)

Buckholme Towers School, Poole

Samuel's Pirate Story

They arrived at the sea. 'There is a good island to explore!' said Spencer to Ellie.

'I like to explore, let's go to the island.'

'Yes,' said Spencer, 'let's see what's on the island. Now let's get our spades to look for treasure,' said Spencer.

'Oh! Look!' said Ellie, 'I have found treasure!'

'Hey, that's my treasure! Come to my pirate ship and walk the plank!' said a pirate.

'Now you have to walk the plank! You should not take a pirate's treasure!'

Calmly Ellie said, 'Now let's go back home.'

Then they went to Ellie's house. 'I hope you've had a good day!' said Spencer.

Samuel Aspland-Monger (6)

Buckholme Towers School, Poole

Paige's Zoo Story

They arrived at the wildlife zoo. Spencer shouted, 'Are you happy?'

Ellie whispered, 'I'm really, really, really happy.'

Then Spencer took Ellie on an elephant. 'This elephant is very slow, please can I get off?' asked Ellie. 'Can I see Pangoa, the panda in the panda jungle?' Ellie asked. 'Hello Pangoa, you are so cute. I wish we could take him with us,' said Ellie. 'Can I go and see the monkey?' asked Ellie.

Then they got off the elephant and went to see the monkey. 'Hello Fifi, please can I have a banana? They look very tasty,' said Ellie.

'I think it is your bedtime,' said Spencer.

'OK,' said Ellie.

'Come on then,' said Spencer.

Paige Olivia Vincent (6)

Buckholme Towers School, Poole

Max's Pirate Story

They arrived at Pirate Island. 'Let's go and find some treasure!' shouted Spencer.
'Let's get digging!' said Ellie. Ellie started to dig, then she hit something. 'Treasure!' shouted Ellie. Then Harry the pirate came onto the island. 'Get me my treasure!' shouted Harry, 'otherwise I will make you walk the Plank of Doom.'
'No!' shouted Ellie. 'This is my treasure!'
'Walk the plank now you scallywags!' said the pirate.
One by one they fell off but two dolphins popped up and saved them. The dolphins took them home. When they got home Ellie went to bed and dreamed about pirates and lots of gold.

Max Bragg (6)
Buckholme Towers School, Poole

Jenson's Pirate Story

They had arrived in a rowing boat. Then they saw land. 'Land ahoy!' yelled Spencer. They rode to the island. They rode closer to Coconut Island.

As they got out of the boat they saw a big box. It glowed in the sunlight. Just at that moment Spencer heard a loud bang and then he pointed to a very big ship.

Then Captain Harry stepped off the boat. 'Give me back my treasure or you will walk the plank!' shouted Harry.

A minute later they were wearing ropes around their hands. Just at that moment they were forced to walk the plank. They had to go step by step. They got closer to the end of the plank. Suddenly, *splash!* They fell into the sea.

Then two big dolphins picked them up. *Splish! Splash!* The dolphins took them home in a flash. Faster and faster, then splished through the waves. They then said goodbye and left. They walked up the path to the little cottage. Spencer said goodbye to Ellie and then Ellie went to bed.

Jenson Hill (6)
Buckholme Towers School, Poole

Latika's Zoo Story

They arrived at the wildlife zoo. Spencer held onto Ellie's hand and they walked through the gate. 'Come on Ellie,' whispered Spencer.

They then saw an elephant. 'Come on Ellie, let's go on the elephant,' said Spencer, so they went on the elephant and had a good ride.

Then they saw a panda called Pango. He was very friendly. Pango loved hugs. He lived in a bamboo jungle. He was the cutest panda in the bamboo jungle.

After that they went back on the elephant. It was very bumpy this time. It was getting very windy, the trees were blowing.

Next they saw a monkey. Then they had some bananas, they were yummy. They then played a game called hide-and-seek. It was fun.

Then Spencer said to Ellie, 'It's time to go home now.' They went back on the elephant and said bye to the monkey. Ellie dreamed about her adventure.

Latika Parmar (6)
Buckholme Towers School, Poole

Siwar's Zoo Story

They arrived at the zoo, there was an elephant at the gate. Ellie and Spencer went through the gate. There were lots of animals.

They saw an elephant and they rode it. Ellie put her teddy on the elephant's trunk, the elephant had bumpy skin. It was grey.

Spencer took Ellie to a panda. The panda was very friendly. Spencer carried the baby panda. The big panda hugged Ellie and her teddy bear.

The elephant took Spencer, Ellie and her teddy bear to look at all of the lovely animals. They were jungle animals. Ellie and Spencer enjoyed it.

At last the elephant took them to an ape. The ape was so kind, he even gave Ellie a banana. Ellie ate lots of bananas. She loved the ape.

Spencer the elf said to Ellie, 'Bye-bye, it's time to go home!' She slept in her bed, dreaming about the zoo. The elephant went back to the zoo.

Siwar Telfah (6)

Buckholme Towers School, Poole

Grainne's Zoo Story

They arrived at the wildlife zoo. 'Oh I hope that we see a monkey!' shouted Ellie. They went through the zoo entrance.

Then they saw an elephant called Fifi. They hopped on Fifi and then they went to see some animals. Ellie hoped to see a monkey.

Then they saw a bamboo forest. Then Spencer said, 'That's where Joe the panda lives and he loves hugs.' They went to see Joe.

Ellie said, 'Oh I hope to see a monkey,' as they went into the monkey cage. 'Yay!' said Ellie, 'there are monkeys!'

Then Ellie said, 'I feel a bit sleepy.' She yawned. Spencer said, 'Let's go home.'

Grainne Davis (6)

Buckholme Towers School, Poole

Ata's Pirate Story

Ellie and Spencer arrived at the beach island. They saw some coconut trees. Ellie whispered, 'I hope there is treasure.'

After that they found treasure, but Spencer saw a pirate ship!

Suddenly the pirate got off his pirate ship. He said, 'Give me that treasure or you will be walking the plank!' But Spencer didn't.

Later the pirate said, 'Walk the plank!' to Spencer and Ellie.

The dolphins saw Spencer and Ellie.

At last Spencer took Ellie home.

Ata John Payne (6)

Buckholme Towers School, Poole

Malachi's Jungle Story

Soon they had arrived in the jungle. They swung through the trees.

Then a snake showed up. It said it wanted to kill them. It had scales.

They ran as fast as they could. 'It is frightening,' said the boy.

They saw a lion. They were a bit frightened. The lion said, 'Don't be frightened.'

They had a ride on his back. They all had fun on the lion's back.

They swung through the trees again. Then they ran into the house. They went upstairs to sleep.

Malachi Jabangwe (6)

Buckholme Towers School, Poole

Maya's Magical Story

Soon they arrived at a meadow and suddenly a unicorn appeared. It said, 'Do you want to go somewhere?'

'Yes please!' they said.

Suddenly a dragon appeared. It started chasing them.

Then they found the unicorn and headed back.

While they were heading back they saw a witch.

Then they pushed the witch away and stole her broomstick to fly home.

Maya Campbell (6)

Buckholme Towers School, Poole

Charlie's Jungle Story

They arrived at the jungle, they swung on vines. It was fun.

They soon came to a snake. It was hungry!

They ran! It was scary.

They found a lion. They were scared.

They rode the lion. It was fun.

They swung back home on the vines.

Charles Allen (7)

Buckholme Towers School, Poole

Dreaming Of Disneyland

Soon, they had arrived at Disneyland, Paris.
Ellie and Spencer came across Anna and Elsa, but
Hans wanted to have dinner with them too!
Elsa froze Hans so she could take Ellie, Spencer
and Anna in her carriage to Rapunzel's tower.
When they arrived, the witch in the tower wanted
them all to leave so Rapunzel slapped her with her
hair and let them down to the ground below. She
swung them all to Ariel's sea palace.
Rapunzel's evil stepmother, the witch, wanted
them gone, so Ariel called her unicorn. The unicorn
took Ellie home to bed and Spencer went home
too.

Emelia Wagstaff (6)
Buckholme Towers School, Poole

Teigan's Pirate Story

They found themselves on a boat. Ellie said, 'Why don't we take a break?'

'OK Ellie. Why, look! An island!' said Spencer.

They went to the island and opened the chest. Inside was a bunch of toys.

In no time Captain Redbeard came. He took them to the boat.

Spencer had to walk the plank. Redbeard said, 'Walk the plank now!'

The dashing dolphins came at last.

Then they got home happily.

Teigan Spry (6)

Charlestown Primary School, St. Austell

Layla's Pirate Story

They found themselves on a rowing boat. Spencer was rowing.

When they got there they found a treasure chest and they opened the lid. Inside were gold bars.

Suddenly Blackbeard stole the treasure chest and took Ellie and Spencer to his boat.

Then Blackbeard made Spencer walk the plank.

Then dolphins came to rescue them.

'It was fun!' said Ellie.

'Yes it was fun,' said Spencer.

Layla Dotty Walby (5)
Charlestown Primary School, St. Austell

Khloe's Pirate Story.

Spencer the elf took Ellie on a paddle boat. They found a desert island.
They found a treasure chest. There were diamonds, jewels and money. There was a pirate on his way.
Blackbeard said, 'I want my treasure chest. Get on my boat.'
'We will,' they said.
The pirate made Spencer walk the plank.
The dolphins saved them.
'We can go home,' said Spencer.

Khloe Chapman (5)
Charlestown Primary School, St. Austell

Dougie's Pirate Story

They arrived on a little rowing boat. Spencer the elf rowed the little rowing boat to a deserted island. When they arrived they found a treasure box.

They opened the chest and they jumped down into the depths into a diamond.

But then a pirate jumped down after them! 'I'm coming for you children!' he said.

The pirate caught the children. Then the pirate climbed back out of the castle and made them walk the plank.

But then two dolphins came to the rescue and saved them.

They walked back to their house and from then on they lived happily ever after.

Dougie Wallace (6)

Charlestown Primary School, St. Austell

Kieran's Pirate Story

There was a tapping at Ellie's window. It was
Spencer. It was time for a trip.
Spencer and Ellie went to an island. Spencer saw a
pirate ship.
The treasure chest was full of food.
Spencer ate the food before the pirate captured
him.
Spencer the elf and Ellie were saved by the
dolphins.
Ellie went home to bed. Ellie said to her teddy, 'It
was fun.'

Kieran James (6)
Charlestown Primary School, St. Austell

Luca's Pirate Story

Spencer the elf and Ellie found themselves in a little rowing boat.
They landed on a desert island. 'Oh no!' said Spencer the elf, 'Redbeard is here!'
Then Redbeard caught them. 'Oh no!' said Ellie.
Then Spencer had to walk the plank.
Then two dolphins came to save the day.
They then went home.

Luca Dominic Vercoe (5)
Charlestown Primary School, St. Austell

Nicky's Pirate Story

Spencer the elf and Ellie found themselves in a little rowing boat.

They rowed the boat, they were heading to a desert island, looking for treasure.

Then a pirate came. He wanted the treasure.

He made Spencer walk the plank and jump in the sea.

Then, in the sea, two dolphins came and saved them.

They then went home.

Nicholas Ling (5)
Charlestown Primary School, St. Austell

Naomi's Pirate Story

They found a boat and rowed to an island.

When they got there Spencer saw a ship and Ellie didn't know.

Redbeard said, 'I want this treasure! Get in my boat!'

They went in the boat. Spencer walked the plank.

Then the dashing dolphins came to save the day.

'We can go home!' said Spencer.

Naomi Squire (6)

Charlestown Primary School, St. Austell

Oliver's Pirate Story

Spencer and Ellie ended up at a desert island.

When they got to the island they found a treasure chest.

'Oh no! A pirate! He's going to capture us!' said Spencer.

He made Spencer walk the plank.

Luckily two dolphins rescued them.

They got to shore and they went home.

Oliver Ferguson (6)

Charlestown Primary School, St. Austell

Millie's Pirate Story

Ellie was asleep when there was a bang on her window. She went on a boat with Spencer the elf. They went on a boat to get to an island.
A pirate came to the island.
The pirate made Spencer walk the plank.
They found some dolphins.
Then they walked home.

Millie Dailey (5)
Charlestown Primary School, St. Austell

Lucas' Pirate Story

They arrived on a boat. Ellie was holding her teddy.
They saw treasure with money.
They saw Blackbeard, he had a sword.
He made them walk the plank.
The dolphins saved them, it was fun.
Soon they were pirates. They went home.

Lucas Woodcock (6)
Charlestown Primary School, St. Austell

Dylan's Pirate Story

They arrived and the little girl was asleep.
They found toys, medals and jewels on the island.
Bluebeard was mad.
Spencer walked the plank.
Two dolphins named Dylan and Dougie came to the rescue.
Then they went home to play.

Dylan Rundle (5)
Charlestown Primary School, St. Austell

Calum's Pirate Story

Spencer and Ellie got on the boat, Spencer and Ellie held her teddy. The sun was shining beautifully.

Ellie was standing on a treasure chest. Jewels and money were in it. Spencer pointed at a pirate ship and Ellie held a crown.

When Blackbeard stepped onto the desert island he was so angry. He waved his sword about and he said, 'Walk the plank!' with a grin. They were scared.

Spencer jumped off the plank, Ellie was so scared but the dolphins saved them. It was windy.

The dolphins caught Ellie and Spencer. Spencer got his wings out. 'What a wonderful day out!' said Ellie.

Calum Matthew Knowles (6)

Charlestown Primary School, St. Austell

Bella's Pirate Story

They found themselves in a rowing boat. Spencer the elf rowed to a treasure island.

Ellie flipped the lid on a treasure chest. Spencer pointed to a pirate ship. Ellie waved but she saw there was a crown.

Redbeard waved his sword. 'Give me my treasure, OK?' he said. 'Get on the ship. Spencer, walk the plank,' said Redbeard.

Ellie and Spencer jumped. Spencer said, 'We need to get back as quick as a flash on these dolphins!' They then got home. 'See you tomorrow,' said Spencer.

Bella Ayling (6)

Charlestown Primary School, St. Austell

Milly's Pirate Story

Spencer knocked on Ellie's window. He said, 'Would you like to go on an adventure with me?'
Ellie was having fun but Spencer saw a pirate ship. 'Look out!' said Spencer, but Ellie didn't hear him. The pirate caught Ellie and Spencer. The pirate wouldn't let the children take the treasure.
The pirate made Spencer walk the plank. He was scared.
Luckily two dolphins saved them. 'Hooray! This is fun!' said Ellie. 'Thank you for the adventure. It was fun.'

Milly Frances Sanders-Hulme (6)
Charlestown Primary School, St. Austell

Lola's Pirate Story

One day Spencer went to visit Ellie's house.
Spencer said, 'Would you like to go on an adventure?'
Ellie said, 'Okay,' so they went. Then they swam.
They swam until they were there.
Finally they got there. They found a treasure chest.
Then a pack of jellyfish came, there was a big one in the middle. They thought that it was the queen and it was. They had a jellyfish kingdom.
'What a good trip out!' said Ellie.

Lola Mae Butters (6)

Charlestown Primary School, St. Austell

Sophie's Pirate Story

They arrived in a rowing boat. Spencer was rowing with the oars. They rowed to a deserted island. They stared at a treasure chest and then they opened it. Then Captain Skull Beard captured them. 'Walk the plank!' he shouted.
Spencer was first to walk the plank. Ellie was terrified.
Then two dancing dolphins carried them across the ocean to their island.
They walked home and Ellie went back into bed.

Sophie Leigh Stoddern (6)
Charlestown Primary School, St. Austell

Isabelle's Pirate Story

They arrived on a desert island.

They found a treasure chest with toys. Spencer saw a pirate ship.

Redbeard had a sword as sharp as a knife. 'Get on my boat! Both of you will walk the plank!'

Luckily the dolphins saved them. They dashed along and took them back to land.

They walked along the path to Ellie's house.

Isabelle Martin (6)

Charlestown Primary School, St. Austell

Amina's Jungle Story

They hopped on her adventure and went to the jungle. They swung on some leafy vines all the way into the deep, dark jungle with the cuddly teddy. Suddenly they met a really mean, slithery snake.

Ellie whispered, 'Wow! A real snake! I have never seen a real snake!'

After a while the slithery snake was really bad so they ran away into the deep, dark woods.

'Run!' shouted Ellie, 'come on Spencer, come on.'

'Wow, a lion! I wonder if the lion is kind or really bad. We don't know do we?' said Spencer.

After the lion turned around and looked at them he said, 'Come and have a ride on my back.'

'What is your name?'

'My name is Wow.'

'Wow, good name.'

'Thanks,' said the nice lion.

'Come on, let's swing on some leafy vines to get back home,' said Ellie.

Amina Marie Moore Webb (7)
King's Park Academy, Bournemouth

Keytlin's Magical Story

They arrived at a candy circus. It was made out of strawberry laces. Then a little pony came. 'Watch out, mean dragons are coming!'

'Don't worry, everything is made out of candy so candyfloss is going to come out,' she said.

'I can't see a thing!' said Spencer.

'That's because of the dragon's candyfloss,' said Ellie.

'I have no friends!' said the dragon.

'Yes you do, you just want to gobble us all up. You won't leave a little tiny bit!' said Ellie.

'Come back you horrible children, you can't come here by yourself. Whoever I see I gobble up. I am so hungry. I won't tell you anymore. I am going to eat you all, come back!' said the dragon.

Suddenly, a unicorn came and saved their lives.

'Thank you,' they said.

'What's that? Let's go see,' said Spencer.

'What is that pointy thing?' asked Ellie.

'I don't know, look! I see lollipops!' said Spencer.

'We are nearly there,' said Spencer.

'Come on, let's go,' said Ellie.

'Do you children want a lollipop?' asked a witch.

'No,' they said.

'Do you want anything?' she said.

'Yes, I just want to go home,' said Ellie.

'Oh, have my broomstick and go home and the elf will bring it back,' said the witch.

'Wow, this thing goes fast!' said Ellie.

Keytlin Zapata (7)
King's Park Academy, Bournemouth

Lincoln's Jungle Story

They arrived at a jungle. They swung from the tickly vines. They swung through the dangerous jungle. They got off and ran quickly. The girl said, 'I can see something in the distance. Let's go and see what it is.'

'Ow! It's a snake!'

'OK, stay very calm, let me go in front,' said the boy, 'let me see if it's a good snake. Hello snake,' the boy said.

The girl said, 'Was it a bad snake?'

'I said hello but he's a bad snake,' said the boy.

'OK run! We need to go now,' said Ellie. They ran quickly.

'Quick or he'll eat you! Now run!' said Spencer. They got so far away. They chopped down a tree. The snake got to the tree and said, 'I'm stuck!'

'Hello, what's your name?' asked Ellie.

'My name is Eddie,' said the snake.

'Hello Eddie, are you friendly?' asked Spencer.

'I am brilliant,' said Eddie.

'A snake was chasing us, our legs are really tired. We can't walk much longer. It's a super long way back,' said Ellie.

The lion gave them a ride. The boy said, 'Look, there's nature. Look there's some vines that lead to our home!'

'Our home! Hooray! I feel glad we're finally here,' said the girl They lived happily ever after.

Lincoln Jack Eldergill (7)

King's Park Academy, Bournemouth

Maja's Magical Story

One sunny day Ellie and Spencer arrived at Magical Land. They found Lola the galloping pony. While Ellie and Spencer were riding Lola, Lola saw something lying on the grass. She pushed back and raced towards the thing lying down on the grass.

Ellie and Spencer fell onto the ground and called, 'Wait! Wait!' but Lola didn't hear them. Suddenly, they heard a fearless dragon and when they turned round they saw one!

They ran as fast as they could and kept saying, 'Run, run as fast as you can, you can't catch me, I'm the gingerbread man!'

When they'd run enough they found Lola and jumped onto her back. Lola gave Ellie a message. It said, 'Candy House!' Ellie and Spencer were starving so they went to the candy house.

When they got there they saw a witch in their way. Spencer said, 'Give us some candy now!'

The nasty witch said, 'No!'

Ellie said, 'Please!'

Then the nasty witch said, 'Okay, but give me two pounds and never come back.'

'Okay,' Ellie and Spencer said.

Whilst they were eating they flew on their broomsticks all the way home to their comfy beds. Ellie said, 'Can we go on another adventure like that Spencer?'
'Okay, maybe next time.'
'Goodnight.' They lived happily ever after.

Maja Grzelczak (7)
King's Park Academy, Bournemouth

Summer's Magical Story

They arrived on a puffy white cloud, they thought they would have a scrumptious picnic. They had some delicious chocolate and strawberry cake with strawberries and water. When they got down to the green, beautiful land they saw a sparkly, glittery unicorn!

Just then they walked into a fierce, terrifying, horrible, ugly dragon and he said, 'Who goes there?'

They couldn't talk one bit because they were so scared. Before they knew it, they were shivering as they never had before in their lives.

They couldn't last any longer so they ran away as fast as they could. Even the fuzzy, cute, little teddy bear was running, he was so scared and terrified so he hid around Ellie's back.

Then they went on the gorgeous, beautiful, elegant, spectacular unicorn and they galloped and saw lots of other things like beautiful flowers.

Just then they saw a small, tiny sign that said:

'Here is Candy Land, you should come; it's delicious and beautiful'.

They went inside. Just when they were exploring Candy Land they saw an evil, ugly, wicked witch. Then she shouted, 'I'm not evil, I'm nice!'

Ellie and Spencer said they were sorry so then she said, 'Do you want to ride on my broom?'
They said, 'Yes.'
Next they were whooshing around and they saw lots of things. Then Spencer dropped Ellie off in the sunny, magnificent morning.

Summer Marie Casserly (7)
King's Park Academy, Bournemouth

Mia's Magical Story

They arrived at the magical enchanted forest. They walked along the path and suddenly they saw a beautiful, graceful unicorn! The unicorn said, 'My name is Emily, would you like to come to my huge, sparkly palace?'

'We would love to,' said Spencer so they climbed on Emily's back and carried on walking on the path. Then they saw a very sleepy dragon! Then Ellie accidently woke up the dragon!

'Oops!' said Ellie. They ran and ran but then they realised that they were running in the wrong direction. They hid behind a tree until the dragon went away. Then they carried on walking.

Then Emily asked, 'Do you want to go to Candy Land first before we go to my palace?'

'Yes,' said Ellie, so Emily teleported to Candy Land, it was full of delicious sweets. Then they saw a path made of the sweetest candyfloss in the world! They walked along the path. Then they suddenly saw a cookie house. They knocked on the door and a witch came out.

'Come in, I am not bad,' said the witch.

They went in and they saw lots of yummy cakes.

'Do you want to ride on my broom?' said the witch.

'Yes,' said Ellie, so they rode on the fantastic broom. Then they lived in Candy Land.

Mia Williams (7)
King's Park Academy, Bournemouth

Jacob's Jungle Story

Soon they had arrived in the wonderful, beautiful, wild jungle. They swung on big, strong, green vines. When they swung on the strong, green, thick vines they had so much fun.

They swung off the big, green, thick vines. They wandered through the big forest. They saw a big, fast, scary snake. The big snake said, 'Do you want to come and have a big, delicious, tasty dinner with me and my friend?'

They got so scared that they ran really, really, really fast. The snake shouted, 'Come back, you look so tasty!'

Ellie said, 'No, I don't want to get eaten, I want to have a big adventure.'

They saw a big, friendly, lovely lion. What a big lion! The lion said, 'Do you want to have a ride on my big, furry back?'

They said, 'Yes, our legs are very, very tired.'

They rode on the big, strong, friendly lion. They were going super fast. They jumped off the lion. The lion said, 'Have a safe journey back home!'

They swung on some big, strong vines. Suddenly they saw home. They swung off the big, green, strong vines. Spencer said, 'Bye!'

Ellie said, 'Bye!' Ellie went home and went to bed.

Jacob mpho Orson (7)

King's Park Academy, Bournemouth

Naomi's Pirate Story

Suddenly they landed on a really, extremely sandy, dusty island. They said, 'Arr me maties, I can see extremely precious and glamorous treasure,' excitedly. They excitedly went to get the precious, glamorous, sparkly treasure.

'Look! Look! Look! An evil, wicked pirate!' said Spencer, worriedly.

'There's no such thing as silly, evil pirates,' said Ellie in a demanding voice. 'So what?' Ellie said 28 times.

However, a scary, fierce, mysterious man called Captain John sadly captured lovely Ellie and special Spencer by waving his spiky, sharp sword about.

'I'm going to throw you onto my dangerous, brown, terrible ship in a second,' said nasty John.

Later horrible Captain John shouted, 'Walk the old plank! Walk the old plank!'

Spencer and Ellie said, 'Okay b-b-boss.' They suddenly felt really clammy when they said it.

However some kind, generous and loving dolphins came above the glistening water to save them.

'Thank you,' said Spencer and Ellie in soft voices. They happily jumped back to Ellie's lovely home.

Naomi Rachel Badger (7)

King's Park Academy, Bournemouth

94

Grace's Magical Story

Ellie and Spencer couldn't believe their eyes. They were filled with enjoyment and amazement. Suddenly, a fire-breathing dragon scared Spencer and Ellie. They ran for their lives. They were spooked by the fire and terrified.

They met a witch. She told them to try one of the yummy lollipops. Ellie said, 'No.'

'Well,' said the witch, 'go away!'

Ellie said no again.

Spencer said, 'You go away!'

Suddenly they fought. Soon Spencer defeated the witch. 'She was vicious,' said Ellie. 'Let's go home, it is late.'

'No,' said Spencer.

'Let's use the boom to go home,' and they did.

Grace Anthony-Ince (7)
King's Park Academy, Bournemouth

Musa's Jungle Story

They arrived at the jungle. They swung on the vines, then they said, 'Yeeha!' They kept on swinging on the vines. It was so fun. They were fearful but it was so delightful. They were so joyful. Suddenly they saw a wriggly snake. Then Spencer said, 'Hello there,' to the snake. They were a bit forgetful and scared, very scared and terrified. They ran as fast as they could, at the speed of a cheetah. They didn't want to stop. They went really fast, superduper fast. They didn't stop.

Then they saw a lion. They were a bit scared. It came out of the bush, it had claws, very sharp claws. He had whiskers, some were long and some were short.

They rode on the lion, it ran very fast, superduper fast.

'This is fun!' said Ellie. It had a long tail and smooth fur. Ellie hugged Spencer, it was fun.

They jumped off the lion and swung on spiky vines. They were going home. They said, 'Yeeha!' The moon was up and they were almost home.

Ellie said, 'Goodbye Spencer!'

Musa Balajo (7)

King's Park Academy, Bournemouth

96

Lily's Pirate Story

They saw a beautiful island in front of the bright sun, so they headed towards the sparkling sun. It was hot and sunny, they sailed and sailed until finally their little wooden boat drifted onto the golden sand of the island.

They wanted to find glittering gold, so they dug up the sand and after one whole hour they were tired. They didn't give up. Soon they found an old wooden treasure chest. But they were soon in big trouble because a pirate came!

The pirate had come to join them, that beast wanted the treasure all for himself. Ellie and Spencer were horrified and fearful! The pirate beast took them and made them walk the plank. They swam through the deep blue sea. They found two grey dolphins.

'Hi,' Spencer said bravely.

'Um... hi,' said Ellie.

'Can you take us home?' asked Spencer.

'Sure,' said the dolphins, so they rode on the dolphins' backs all the way home.

Lily Tebboth (7)
King's Park Academy, Bournemouth

Alicja's Magical Story

Ellie asked, 'Where are we going?'

'We are going to Magical Land,' said Spencer.

They soon arrived at Magical Land. Suddenly a green fearless dragon came out and blew red and orange fire from his smelly mouth. They said, 'Oh no!'

They ran really quickly but the fearless dragon was too quick. He was breathing fire, everything was black and burnt.

Finally they found their magic unicorn. They said, 'This is painful.' They galloped slowly towards the lollipops.

Suddenly a witch popped out. Ellie didn't care, she just ate the yummy, delicious lollipops. They ran and found an old, dusty broomstick.

They safely went home. They saw lots of unicorns and colourful, yummy lollipops. Ellie said, 'Can we go there next time?'

'Yes,' answered Spencer.

Alicja Lewandowska (7)

King's Park Academy, Bournemouth

Zalaa's Magical Story

They arrived at the magical forest. They walked along the yellow brick path. Then they saw a beautiful, lovely, graceful unicorn. She said, 'Would you like to see the beautiful forest?'
'Of course we do, don't we Ellie?'
'Um yes.'
Suddenly Spencer the elf accidentally poured cold water onto the unicorn and she turned into a fierce dragon. It nearly burnt Spencer and Ellie. Ellie had juice in her backpack. Ellie threw the juice onto the fiery dragon.
Then the dragon turned into a green, slimy, gooey witch. The witch tried to make fire and candy, she couldn't make fire but luckily she could make sweet candy. Ellie and Spencer threw candy at the mean witch.
The mean witch was so slimy that she melted into a tiny nibbling rabbit. The witch forgot her rough, hard broom. The rabbit had the magic star wand and it could talk. Then all of Ellie's family came onto the broom.
They had a hot campfire. They all had pizza and after that they had marshmallows. They tasted fabulous. Then they magically went back home.

Zalaa Shinwari (7)
King's Park Academy, Bournemouth

99

Caleb's Pirate Story

They arrived in a rowing boat on the wavy sea. When Spencer turned around he saw a hot, sandy desert island so they quickly rowed to the refreshing desert island.

When they got there they suddenly saw a golden and wooden treasure chest. Ellie found a crown. She said, 'I want to give this to Dave, my teddy!'

'That's mine me hearties!' said a voice. They turned around and saw a pirate. He introduced himself. He said, 'I may be the best of all captains, Captain Buckleboots.'

Spencer said, 'Why don't you share?'

Buckleboots shouted, 'No! You will walk the plank or else!' So Spencer started to walk the creaky plank.

A diving dolphin saved him so Ellie walked into the water. *Whoosh!* A dolphin saved her and Dave. But it was night-time, time for bed, so Captain Spencer, Dave and Ellie walked home in the shining, sparkly moonlight.

Caleb Morrison (7)

King's Park Academy, Bournemouth

Jessica's Zoo Story

Once upon a time there lived a girl called Ellie and an elf called Spencer. She woke up because of a tap on her window. It was Spencer the elf. He said, 'Do you want to come on an adventure with me?' She said, 'Yes please! Of course I will come.' Then they arrived at the zoo.

First they saw the elephant at the gates and they got on her back. They rode on her back.

Next they saw the big, fat bear. They were sad that the big fat bear took their teddy bear off them.

After that they went back on the elephant. They rode to the next animal.

Next they saw the monkey eating a tasty banana. The bear was on a wire and the children ate tasty bananas.

Suddenly they got back on the elephant's back and she took Ellie back to her house. Spencer said, 'Goodbye beautiful Ellie!'

Jessica Pardy (7)

King's Park Academy, Bournemouth

Rihanna's Jungle Story

One day there was a funny boy and a beautiful girl swinging through the wonderful, colourful water jungle.

Then they saw a shifty, scaly, scary snake and then the snake said, 'How are you today?'

The snake quickly chased after them as quick as he could. He was like a fast cheetah. The kids were screaming, 'Argh! Help me please! Help please!'

They met the nice, kind, wonderful, bright, colourful lion. The children said, 'Are you a nice, good lion?'

The lion said, 'Yes of course I am.'

Then the lion said, 'Do you want a ride?'

The children said, 'Oh yes please, that would be so wonderful of you!' Then they swung home as fast as they could on the fat brown ropes.

Rihanna Jordan Banes (7)

King's Park Academy, Bournemouth

Olivia's Magical Story

Once an amazing girl called Ellie silently woke up and found Spencer the elf. Ellie said, 'Oh, hi Spencer.'

Spencer said, 'Do you want to go on an adventure?'

Ellie said, 'OK.' Then they flew silently. There were no words.

Then they got to ride the pony. They rode and rode. Then they got to a dragon and it stared at Ellie. They both ran. Ellie said to the dragon, 'Go and run!' She shouted loudly and the dragon did. Then they rode and rode quicker. They met a witch who said, 'Would you like a magic mop?'

Ellie said, 'OK.'

Then they flew to Ellie's house and she got into bed. Then Spencer zoomed back to where he lived.

Olivia Aitken (6)
King's Park Academy, Bournemouth

Liam's Pirate Story

They arrived at a desert island. They saw an 'X'
marking the spot. They dug it up and there was
shiny gold.

'Hey, that's my treasure!' said a pirate. Then a
cannonball was shot at them. A pirate said, 'Do
you want to be in our crew?'

'Yes,' said the boy and girl.

'Tricked you! Walk the plank!' said the pirate.

'OK!' they said. *Splash! Splash!*

Then they got a ride on the fantastic dolphins.
Then they went home and had some chocolate
and a cup of tea.

Liam Clark (6)
King's Park Academy, Bournemouth

Callum's Space Story

They arrived in the deep, dark, beautiful space. They found a moon called Murcklry to land on but Ellie wanted some stars.

'We'll go and get some then,' said Spencer. But they only got one star. Ellie and Spencer went to find something to use it on.

After a while they found a treasure chest. They used the star to unlock the humongous brown chest to get lots of coins. Then they flew away.

Just then a UFO came and sucked Ellie up! She was scared. The UFO flew with Spencer in it as well. Ellie told the super green alien, 'This is fun!' The UFO went really fast. Spencer had to hold onto the glass. Soon Spencer fell asleep, Ellie was wide awake.

Suddenly there was a huge jellyfish with a spectacular tongue. Its tongue was eight thousand times bigger than human peachy-pink tongues.

Soon Ellie wanted to go home. Spencer asked Ellie, 'Do you want to go home?'

Ellie exclaimed, 'Yes!' Ellie went home so she could go to bed and go to sleep.

Callum Jones (7)

King's Park Academy, Bournemouth

Vanessa's Magical Story

They arrived at a magical, colourful world. Jojo Bear was confused, he was asleep the whole time. They met a kind, wise, sweet and fearless unicorn. She told them that she was going to help them. Soon they got blocked by a fiery red dragon! He was sleeping, he was quiet. Aitchoo! went Jojo, then the dragon woke up!

Uni the unicorn ran away, leaving the two children alone. They ran as fast as they could and they got away but he caught up with them. He shot eight fire blades at them, then nine, ten, eleven, twelve and thirteen. Then he went back home to his calm, lovely mummy.

He spread his wings and said in a booming voice, 'You should come to mine for tea so we can play catch.'

'OK.' Overhead they saw Uni, she took them and dropped them at Chocolate Hilltop. Ellie and Spencer walked to a house but they ran into an old, greasy witch. She offered them a lolly each. She said they are sweets but they were poisonous. They said no but she stuffed them in their mouths. They had a drink and stole her broom and flew away.

They flew home and had a delicious breakfast of pancakes, berries and cookies. Spencer got to stay over. They had fun. They played trains, teachers, bakery, sleeping lions and they painted. Spencer said that he was going to take her on another adventure.

He said that he'd take her to Elf Land to see his family and friends or they'd go visit Mr Dragon and play catch.

Vanessa Kate Muzanenhamo (7)

King's Park Academy, Bournemouth

Shahid's Space Story

They arrived in outer space. 'Cool!' said Ellie, 'this is the best day!' They saw all the stars and collected some. 'When do we go home?' They were lost, Ellie didn't know.

Spencer the elf held the stars. Suddenly, an alien came! He was going to trap Ellie and Spencer in his flying saucer! They were on the moon!

The alien was going to trap them but he only trapped Ellie with her teddy. He wasn't a bad alien. He was a good alien. He had more friends in his flying saucer.

His friends were friendly too. They had flying saucers. They zoomed through the world and showed them around space. They waved to all of the people.

A moon monster came, he had a long, pink, huge tongue. They were surprised to see him! He had sharp teeth and three eyes.

They went down and Ellie went home. She went home and waved goodbye to the alien and Spencer the elf! It was nearly night-time so she went to her house.

Shahid Mahmoodi (7)
King's Park Academy, Bournemouth

Maud's Magical Story

Ellie was filled with joy and excitement but they couldn't believe their eyes when they saw twinkling fairies flying across to Fairy Land. Suddenly, a terrifying, dreadful dragon came up and saw Ellie and Spencer.

The terrifying, scary dragon was trying to eat up Spencer and Ellie but they ran away just in time. After that they ran all the way to find a unicorn so they could go faster to get away from the dragon. Then they finally found a unicorn, it was the same unicorn as the last one they were on so they knew it could fly. They touched its horn and they were gone.

They'd flown enough. They flew down and saw a cruel, wicked witch. She was going to put them in a cage. They both said, 'Get me out of here!' After that Teddy hid, he got them out. They took the broom, then they quickly got the key and they left the house.

They flew to Ellie's house and went back to bed.

Maud Lowe (6)
King's Park Academy, Bournemouth

Greta's Pirate Story

They arrived in a small boat and sailed carefully until Spencer saw a golden sandy island. They sailed and sailed and they finally arrived at the island.

The sand was golden and they found a chest of silver and gold. Suddenly, a mean pirate ship sailed towards them.

An angry pirate called Captain Redbeard went off the ship. He was so angry he shouted, 'You are walking the plank, both of you are doing that!'

They both went onto his disgusting and dirty ship but Spencer didn't worry at all because he saw a little dolphin at the side. *They are to going to save us!* he thought and they did!

They splashed beautifully all the way through until they got home to the fantastic and wonderful land. They went home, it was just in time for delicious breakfast. It was yummy pancakes and Ellie gave Spencer some too. He loved it.

Greta (7)

King's Park Academy, Bournemouth

Maison's Space Story

After flying for many hours they gently touched down on the moon's surface.

Ellie and Spencer started to collect shiny, silvery, gold stars. Then Ellie and Spencer found a colourful rocket so they both flew to burning hot Mars. It was hotter than the sun.

Then they met a space vampire. The vampire was very scary. He trapped Ellie and Spencer. They were both trapped for an eternity. They managed to escape with a sharp pickaxe.

The terrifying vampire got stuck in a yellow crater whilst jumping really high. He was stuck in there forever.

Then they found a magnificent alien who was silly. His name was Blobby Junior. They said bye to Blobby Junior.

Then the magic elf dropped the girl off. Ellie got back into bed before daytime.

Maison Walkinshaw (7)
King's Park Academy, Bournemouth

Rubie's Magical Story

One sunny day Ellie and Spencer arrived at Wonderland. Ellie and Spencer had flown to Wonderland and they found a beautiful pony. They rode the pony.

Suddenly they saw a big, giant, fire-breathing dragon. It came towards them. Suddenly the dragon started to scare the children.

'Run from the dragon!' shouted Spencer.

Finally they got away and they found the wonderful pony from when they were first in Wonderland.

Suddenly they saw a house made of sweets. A witch came out of the house and said, 'Go away!' So they ran away. When they ran away they took a broomstick with them.

Ellie felt happy at the end of the adventure because she got to see some unicorns and she got to take one home with her.

Rubie Barnes (7)

King's Park Academy, Bournemouth

Leyla's Magical Story

They arrived at a sweetie magical circus. They saw a unicorn doing tricks while a dragon came and blew fire at the unicorn. She screamed, ran out and found a spooky house.

In that house lived another spooky, ugly, scary, terrifying dragon! It was aiming fire at the unicorn but the fire was candyfloss.

Ellie and Spencer ran away as fast as they could! Then they got back on the graceful unicorn and they found an ugly, greedy wizard. The wizard gave Spencer and Ellie nothing so then they got back on the beautiful unicorn and found a massive palace that was huge.

Suddenly they heard a big *bang!* They both said, 'Woah!' Soon they found another greedy wizard that gave just the little brown bear a lolly. The clever children got mad at the wizard and tried to snatch the lollies off the wizard.

Finally they found a flying broom so they climbed on it and they flew home. They had a delicious dinner of spaghetti and delicious meatballs. After they had chocolate ice cream.

Leyla Tuanna Kilic (6)
King's Park Academy, Bournemouth

Nasrine's Magical Story

One night a really sneaky elf said, 'Do you want to go on a great adventure?'
Ellie said, 'I would love to because I have always dreamed of going on a great adventure.'
Suddenly they saw a sign that said: 'Magical Land'. They ran quickly as fast as they could because they were so excited to see what was inside.
Suddenly they saw a fearless dragon. They ran as fast as they could, the dragon was too late. He roared loudly. They couldn't believe what they'd seen. They both said, 'You are so pretty.'
They met a really sneaky witch and Spencer and Ellie were laughing because she'd lost all of her old teeth. She only had one tooth in her smelly and slimy mouth. They saw something behind her. They ran as fast as they could. Ellie got back safely to her cuddly bed.

Nasrine Tir (7)

King's Park Academy, Bournemouth

Ugnius' Space Story

Ellie was filled with excitement, she couldn't believe that she was in space! There were 10 beautiful stars. The stars were sparkling yellow. When they flew out to space it was dark as a bat.

Ellie and Spencer landed on the giant, sparkly, glorious moon. They collected three sparkly yellow stars. There was a green alien hiding with a little laugh on the moon.

The green alien caught Ellie in his spaceship and he caught her teddy. It was scary for Ellie to go in the metal and wooden unbreakable spaceship. Then they flew to see the stars.

Ellie looked out the window with her teddy and the green alien. Ellie touched the window of the spaceship. Suddenly, there was a monster with a long tongue on the moon. Ellie was shocked at what she saw on the moon.

Suddenly she flew home in the green alien's spaceship.

Ugnius Stankus (7)

King's Park Academy, Bournemouth

Valentina's Space Story

Ellie was filled with amazement because it was her dream to go into space, she was in magic space where the sky was not black and the stars were not twinkly. The sky was purple and the stars were such a treat.

Then Spencer saw a horrifying, monstrous monster who would like to eat anything!

Meanwhile, Ellie was frightened so much that she went onto the next planet. Suddenly, the dreadful monster went into his space rocket and spied on the peculiar children.

Then a lolly alien came. It trapped the children and the children said, 'Please get me out of here!' But the witch was so, so, so mean that she wouldn't even let them drink or eat.

Then their unicorn came and saved them. After that they went back to their normal, fun, spectacular house.

Valentina Vallejos (7)

King's Park Academy, Bournemouth

Meyra's Magical Story

Soon they had arrived at a place called the Fairy Magic Land. There was a magical unicorn. They hopped onto her to discover more.

Soon they saw a fire-breathing dragon. Spencer and Ellie ran away because it breathed fire.

They ran away quickly because they wanted to stay safe. Then they were safe because the dragon was far away.

An hour later Spencer and Ellie hopped onto the magical unicorn and it clip-clopped away to the gingerbread house.

When they got there they ate all of the candy. The witch appeared and said, 'Why are you eating my candy?' When the witch was not looking they stole her magic broom and flew back home. The witch said, 'Get back you two! You stole my candy!'

Meyra Guler Acik (7)
King's Park Academy, Bournemouth

Lucy's Magical Story

Once upon a time there was a little kind girl named Ellie and a funny elf named Spencer. They travelled somewhere called Fairy Land of Business. They went on a magical pony.

They saw a fierce dragon who breathed fierce fire. They were fearful. They ran as fast as they could. The fierce dragon tripped over a stony rock and accidentally breathed fire.

Then they got safely back to their magical, nice, safe place. They rode in woods until they saw a house full of candy. Then they shouted, 'Candy!' Then an old, grumpy witch came out and said, 'Don't you eat my candy!'

Then they saw a broomstick and the teddy bear was falling off it. They then got home safely.

Lucy Downton (7)
King's Park Academy, Bournemouth

Leo's Magical Story

One bright sunny day there was a magical elf, he had fairytale tickling dust. The smart elf had a beautiful friend called Ellie. She saw a wicked witch. She had the biggest sparkly monster called Ben so they ran away.

The witch did a spell and the spell took them to a massive, strange prison. The prison was made out of massive bricks.

'Wow, get on and I will take you to a palace.' The mean ghost locked up the queen and the king. The ghost said, 'Nobody will get out of here.'

The elf found a key and the queen and king said, 'Thank you for being kind, I hope you have a lovely night with your sister and your mate and 100 friends.'

Leo George Bekir (7)
King's Park Academy, Bournemouth

Antonia's Magical Story

Ellie was filled with joy and excitement because she went to the magical land with Spencer. Ellie couldn't believe how fantastic it was. There were glittery fairies sprinkling rainbow, magical dust. Suddenly they saw a rainbow coloured unicorn. Ellie wanted to go on the unicorn.
Then they saw a red and black fire dragon. It was terrifying them.
'What is it?' said Ellie. How scary it was! It shot fire out from its mouth.
They ran away from the dragon because it shot fire. They ran away silently and the magic teddy ran too. They were really frightened.
They got on the unicorn to go back home. Before they went home they got magic dust.

Antonia Elcock (7)
King's Park Academy, Bournemouth

Jana's Zoo Story

Once upon a time they went to the zoo. The elephant was hiding because he liked jumping out on the people. The little girl was called Ellie. The elf was called Spencer. Then the elephant said, 'Do you want a ride?'

Ellie said, 'Yes, we want to go to the pandas.'

It was a long way there. The pandas were really cuddly and soft too. The baby was so cute.

Next they rode on, there were lots of green leaves. They went to the monkey. Ellie ate a lot of bananas.

'Don't eat my last banana because that is my favourite,' said the monkey. They'd had a wonderful time there.

Jana Anna Zirne (7)
King's Park Academy, Bournemouth

Millie's Zoo Story

Ellie and Spencer arrived at the zoo. Ellie had never been to the zoo before. They were very excited.

A huge elephant lifted Ellie and Spencer carefully up onto his huge back and trotted off through the zoo.

First they visited the cuddly panda. The panda put down her cuddly panda cub. She grabbed Ellie's teddy bear. Spencer picked up the panda cub.

The elephant Ellie and Spencer up onto his huge back again. Then they visited the hungry gorilla and they ate bananas together. Ellie and Spencer were so happy.

He lifted Ellie and Spencer up onto his back and dropped Ellie off at home.

Millie Taylor (7)
King's Park Academy, Bournemouth

Joanna's Jungle Story

Ellie and Spencer were swooping through the leafy vines. Ellie knew lots about the jungle. How did she know all of those things? What an amazing girl she was! Spencer asked, 'Which way do we go?'
Ellie said, 'That way.'
Suddenly a horrible, dangerous and fierce snake appeared out of nowhere and chased them.
Speedily they got out of the cave and met a lion called Harry. He said, 'Hello!' He was frightened about what was going to happen next.
Harry showed Ellie and Spencer around and after that perfect day Harry took them safely back home.

Joanna Maru (7)
King's Park Academy, Bournemouth

Amber's Pirate Story

One spooky night Spencer and Ellie sat in a little tiny boat and Spencer said, 'We're nearly at Sprindes Island.'
Suddenly they saw a pirate treasure chest.
Eventually Spencer saw a gigantic ship. Then Ellie's teddy came to life.
Eventually the peglegged pirate took them to his really messy pirate ship. Then the pirate said, 'Ahoy there me hearties!' The huge pirate told Spencer to walk the plank. The rude pirate shouted, 'Walk the plank! Walk the plank!'
Then Ellie and Spencer rode dolphins home.

Amber Moors (7)
King's Park Academy, Bournemouth

Patryk's Zoo Story

First they went to the funny zoo and Ellie thought that the elephant was going to jump on them. Suddenly the elephant took them on a zoo trip to see the pandas. When they went to the pandas they were cute.

Then they went on another trip and the elephant held the bear with his trunk.

'Wow! A gorilla! This is the best day ever!' said Ellie. The gorilla was black.

Then they finally went home. What a busy day it was at the funny zoo.

Patryk Wieczorek (6)
King's Park Academy, Bournemouth

Roxy's Jungle Story

Ellie felt the wind blowing through her hair. When they got down they met a slithery snake. He wanted to eat them.

Ellie, Spencer and the bear ran away from the slithery snake. Then they met a nice lion. Spencer said to the lion, 'My friend needs to get home. Can we ride on your back?'

'Of course,' he said.

It was very exciting. The lion was very soft and super fast. Then they swung on the vines to get back home.

Roxy Hardman (7)
King's Park Academy, Bournemouth

Alfie's Jungle Story

Ellie swung on spiky vines attached to a huge tree. Suddenly, she saw a huge, stripy green, black and scaly snake. Its hiss was really scary. They ran away quickly.

Then a green crocodile popped up and swallowed Ellie but she was OK.

They met a yellow furry lion. He was very kind. They jumped on the lion's back and had a bumpy ride.

Then they went home.

Alfie Jhon Maunder (7)
King's Park Academy, Bournemouth

Chloe's Pirate Story

Ellie and Spencer went on a boat. Spencer was rowing it.

Ellie and Spencer saw a pirate. Spencer pointed at Ellie and Teddy had a crown. A fearless pirate stole the treasure, it was Ellie and Spencer's chocolate coins.

The pirate made them walk the plank into the sea. Ellie rode a dolphin in the sea. Then they went back home and had fun.

Chloe Forbes (7)

King's Park Academy, Bournemouth

Grace's Magical Story

Ellie and Spencer the elf found a princess unicorn named Grace. Suddenly, Grace dropped Ellie and Spencer off at a maze cave.

Then a huge, colourful and fierce dragon appeared. Ellie found a secret way out of the creepy maze cave. Grace was sleeping outside of the maze cave. Spencer said, 'Wake up.'

Grace quickly and quietly trotted away and came to a lovely place. Ellie and Spencer went to a nasty witch's candy house. Spencer and Ellie ate some of it. The nasty witch became best friends with them. Ellie and Spencer went home.

Grace Wigmore (7)

King's Park Academy, Bournemouth

Nataliya's Space Story

Ellie was happy that she was in space. There were some burning hot stars.
Aliens abducted Teddy. Ellie cried, 'Spencer!' Then an alien waved his tongue at the big green alien's spaceship. He had spots.
Spencer took Ellie home. Ellie waved at the alien spaceship. He flew off to Mars and Jupiter.

Nataliya Marguerite Le Notre (7)
King's Park Academy, Bournemouth

130

Heidi's Jungle Story

They went to a jungle full of snakes, they soon found vines so they swung on them. They were so excited! Then one snake slithered up the vines. They said, 'Uh oh!' because the snake wrapped around Ellie. A panda saved them.

'Yay!' they said.

They just managed to escape from the snake. The snake just kept hissing and hissing until they got to a tall tree.

They made friends with a terrified lion. The lion was so happy that he had friends. They nearly played with him all night.

Then the lion took them to some tall vines and he helped them up the tall, tall, tall vines.

They swung on the tall, tall, tall vines and went to their snuggly house.

Heidi Ainge (6)
Priestley Primary School, Calne

Riley's Jungle Story

They arrived at a stinky swamp with crocodiles, piranhas, fish and ogres.

Suddenly a huge crocodile jumped out of the water with piranhas and a horrifying snake slithered down a tree.

They grabbed a branch and put it in the crocodile's nasty mouth. It got stuck and the crocodile couldn't gobble them up.

Later, they found a lion. They thought it might eat them but when they got to know him they thought, *he won't eat us up.*

They hopped onto the lion and he led them home. Then they stopped.

Then they swung all the way home.

Riley Ewart George Green (7)

Priestley Primary School, Calne

Elliott's Jungle Story

They arrived in a green and brown jungle with a snake and ferocious bears. When they landed they swung on very strong branches. Soon they landed on a beautiful tree.

They saw a slimy snake and it was creepy. The snake surrounded them. The snake was very bad. Both Ellie and Spencer ran from the snake because he was going to eat them.

Then they saw a lion. He smiled at them. It was a wild lion.

They rode on the lion. It was a long ride. It was so fun and then they stopped.

They swung on two vines, then they walked home.

Elliott Mouillé (6)
Priestley Primary School, Calne

Ffion's Jungle Story

They arrived in a jungle full of erupting volcano and red-hot lava.
Soon they bumped into a terrifying snake. The snake hissed at them!
They ran away from the snake super fast! They lost him!
Soon they saw a lion, they thought it would eat them but luckily he didn't.
They had a super bumpy ride on the friendly lion.
Then they swung home once more.

Ffion Simpkins (6)
Priestley Primary School, Calne

Abigail's Jungle Story

They arrived in a hot, smelly, hairy jungle. Teddy got caught on a thorn and Teddy's stuffing was coming out!

They bumped into a friendly snake and it was a direction snake.

The snake directed them to a ferocious lion! It was actually a friendly lion when he got to know them. Then the lion gave them a really quick ride.

They then went home on the thorny vines. They had a campfire and they roasted marshmallows.

Abigail Wright (6)
Priestley Primary School, Calne

135

The Storyboards

Here are the fun storyboards
children could choose from...

MAGICAL ADVENTURE

JUNGLE TALE

PIRATE ADVENTURE

SPACE STORY

ZOO ADVENTURE